For Abdulla
K.L.
For Max
V.W.

With thanks to Ifrah and
the whole of the Harrow EMAS team
and to the children of
Little Stanmore First & Middle School,
Norbury School and
Vaughan First & Middle School

Abdi	*Ilyas*	*Phoebe*
Abdirahman	*Harun*	*Ruwayda*
Abdulahi	*Kareem*	*Saied*
Amber	*Lydia*	*Sanjar*
Delia	*Majurhan*	*Sharon*
Fatima	*Maya*	*Stacey*
Gabrielle	*Mohammed*	*Suhur*
Hamda	*Mustafe*	*Troy*
Hibo	*Oyinda*	*Wais*

Abdi's house was quiet.
Everybody was asleep.

Abdi leaped out of bed and
ran across the hall.
"Wake up everybody!" he shouted.
"Wake up! I don't want to be late!"

"Not so loud Abdi,"
grumbled Dad. "Calm down!"

"Today is the school trip,"
shouted Abdi.
"The trip to the seaside!"

Dad hurried into the kitchen to make anjeero for breakfast.

"Is my picnic ready?" said Abdi. "Miss Ryan said to bring two sandwiches, a drink and some fruit."

Mrs Ali packed
four cheese sandwiches.
She added four tuna sandwiches.
Then she put in two apples,
two pears, four drinks and
some anjeero.

"Mum! That's too much food. I will be sick!"
"Don't eat it all at once, Abdi…
and you can share. Maybe your friends
would like some anjeero."

"Have fun!" said Dad. "Don't forget
your waterproof jacket. It always rains at the seaside!"
Then he ran off to catch the bus.

Mrs Ali bundled baby Ayan into her buggy and
they rushed down the road.

"Just in time!" said Miss Ryan.
"Here's your name badge Abdi.
We don't want you to get lost!"

"Do you lose children on these trips?" asked Mrs Ali.
"No, of course not! Abdi will be fine.
I will make sure he stays near me all day."
Abdi groaned.

"Line up children, please,"
said Miss Ryan.

"The coach should be here soon,"
said Mr Yin the teaching assistant.

"Miss! I need to go…
I really do!" moaned Samira,
crossing her legs.
"Me too!" said Katie.
"And me," said Kai.

Tim's mum looked scared.
She stood at the door of the bus
and waved and waved.

"He has never been away on his own!" she said. "Don't worry," said Miss Ryan. "Abdi will help me look after him. We will all be back this evening... safe and sound."

The day was bright and sunny.
Abdi and Tim waved to the cars on the road.

Some naughty children pulled funny faces at the drivers.

Samira made a funny face too. "I feel sick!" she groaned.
Mr Yin, the teaching assistant stuck a sick bag under her chin.

Then her friend Anna was sick too.

The coach left the motorway and
drove for miles through beautiful little villages,
past enormous fields with lazy, grazing cows.

Then Abdi saw it.
"There it is!" he shouted. "The sea! I saw it first!"
"No, I did! I saw it first!" shouted Tim
"It's so wide," said Samira.
She was feeling much better.

The bus parked by the beach.
Everyone got off and the fun began.

"I'm going to Australia!"
shouted Abdi.
"Me too!" said Tim.
They were disappearing
down a deep hole.
"I promised your mums
to bring you boys home,"
said Miss Ryan.
"You can go to Australia
another time."

Everyone played happily
until Miss Ryan shouted, "LUNCHTIME!"

Abdi opened his big bag of food.
Tim leaned over to look.

He tripped and
dropped all his sandwiches
in the sand and
then squashed them.

"Don't worry, Tim.
I have got loads,"
said Abdi.

He shared his huge feast with
Tim, Mohammed and Samira.

After lunch, a football game started.

When the match ended,
Miss Ryan could not find Abdi.
"Has anyone seen Abdi?" she asked.
But no-one knew where he was.

The children looked behind the deck chairs.
They looked under the beach huts.

They looked in the shop.
But Abdi was not there.

Then Tim came racing up the beach.
"Abdi found a kite," he said.
"Look, there's one up there!"

Miss Ryan looked up and
then she looked down.
There was Abdi, a long way away.

Miss Ryan ran along the sand.
"Abdi," she shouted.
"You should not run off like that.
It's not safe. We were worried.
Come on. It's time
to go home."

"Sorry, Miss Ryan," said Abdi.
"The kite pulled me."

The drive back was quiet.

At the school gate,
the mums and dads were waiting.
Tim's mum was smiling.

"It was brilliant, Dad!" said Abdi.
"And it didn't rain. Can we go again tomorrow?"
"Maybe not tomorrow, but soon," said Dad.

Anjeero

Anjeero is a flat bread with a slightly spongy texture
that is eaten in Somalia and neighbouring countries.
To make anjeero, flour is mixed with water and yeast and allowed
to sit for several days until it ferments. Fermentation happens when yeast (a tiny
living fungus) feeds on flour and it is what gives anjeero its slightly sour taste.
The liquid batter (like pancake batter) is traditionally cooked on a clay plate
placed over a fire. It can also be poured into a pan and cooked on a stove.

In the morning, anjeero may be eaten with butter and honey or lemon.
At other meals, anjeero is used to scoop up stews and salads.

This book was produced for Harrow Ethnic Minority Achievement Service
in partnership with the Somali community and schools and teachers in Harrow and
is a story with which all children can engage.